WEEKLY WR READER

EARLY LEARNING LIBRARY

This Is My Story

I Come from Ivory Coast

by Valerie J. Weber

Reading consultant: Susan Nations, M.Ed., author/literacy coach/
consultant in literacy development

Please visit our web site at: www.garethstevens.com
For a free color catalog describing Weekly Reader® Early Learning Library's list
of high-quality books, call 1-877-445-5824 (USA) or 1-800-387-3178 (Canada).
Weekly Reader® Early Learning Library's fax: (414) 336-0164.

Library of Congress Cataloging-in-Publication Data available upon request from publisher.
Fax (414) 336-0157 for the attention of the Publishing Records Department.

ISBN-10: 0-8368-7236-3 — ISBN-13: 978-0-8368-7236-1 (lib.bdg.)
ISBN-10: 0-8368-7243-6 — ISBN-13: 978-0-8368-7243-9 (softcover.)

This edition first published in 2007 by
Weekly Reader® Early Learning Library
A Member of the WRC Media Family of Companies
330 West Olive Street, Suite 100
Milwaukee, WI 53212 USA

Copyright © 2007 by Weekly Reader® Early Learning Library

Art direction: Tammy West
Cover design, page layout, and maps: Charlie Dahl

Photography: All photos © Steve Winter Photography

Printed in the United States of America

1 2 3 4 5 6 7 8 9 10 09 08 07 06

Table of Contents

Cover and title page: I like to swing at the park near my dad's house!

Two Countries, Two Names

Hi! My name is Neneh Karen, and I am nine years old. I come from Ivory Coast, a country in western Africa. Now I live in New York City. My American friends call me "Karen." When I talk to other Africans, I like to be called "Neneh." *Neneh* means "mother" in the Fulani (FOO-lah-nee) language. Fulani is one of the hundreds of languages spoken in Africa.

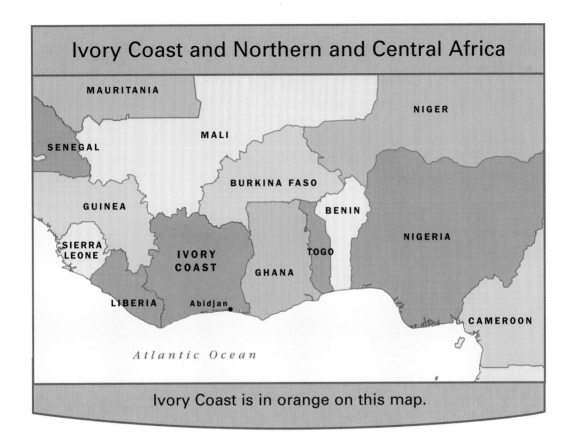

Ivory Coast is in orange on this map.

The **official** name for Ivory Coast is in French — Côte d'Ivoire (COAT dee-VWAR). French is the official language of my **homeland**. I lived with my grandparents and my uncle in Abidjan (ah-bee-JAHN), the biggest city in Ivory Coast. Their big house is close to the beach. Ivory Coast has many beautiful beaches, forests, **grasslands**, and modern cities.

Here is a picture of my dad, my cousin Kanou, me, and my mom. Kanou came to live with me a few months ago.

Eighteen months ago, I moved to New York City to be with my mom and my dad. I also left Ivory Coast because people were fighting in Abidjan. They burned down my school.

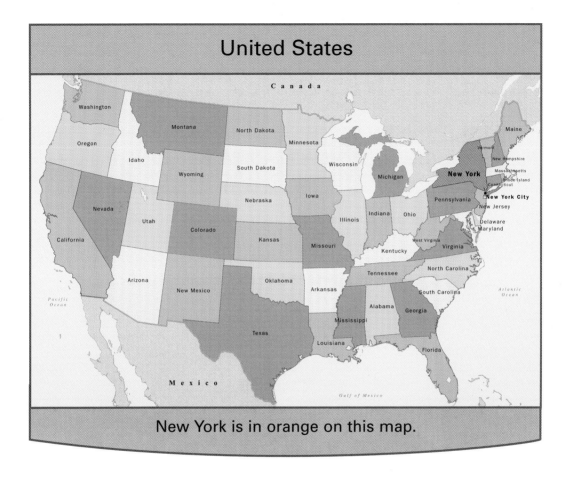

United States

New York is in orange on this map.

I moved to New York in the winter. What a shock! It is always pretty warm in Ivory Coast. New York can be very cold in the winter and very hot in the summer. I was so happy the first time it snowed here. I had wanted to see snow for so long. Now snow is no big deal. It is just frozen water!

A Taste of Africa in New York

New York City is the biggest city in the United States. People from all over the world move here. We can get anything we need in New York. We can eat at African restaurants. We can buy **ingredients** to cook African food at home.

We can even rent or buy African movies! This store rents only African movies.

When we lived in Ivory Coast, sometimes we ate at a table, and sometimes we sat on the floor. My mom would put a large bowl with our food in it on the floor. My family all sat around the bowl, dipping into it with a spoon or with their hands. People often eat this way in Africa.

We are sharing a stew from **Senegal** called tieboudien (TEE-ay-boo-djen) at this African restaurant. It is made from fish, rice, and vegetables and is very **spicy**.

One of my favorite African foods is attieke (ah-tee-AY-kay). It is made from pounded yams. I also like cooked **plantains**, grilled chicken, or fish with rice. In New York, I love the hamburgers at fast-food restaurants.

Whether I am in Ivory Coast or New York, I love pizza!

My cousin Kanou was born in the United States. She is almost eight years old. I like to teach her games from Africa.

We have our own handclapping game in Africa. Children in the United States play a similar game.

Some African people in New York wear their **traditional** clothes from their homeland. My Auntie Oumou wears her traditional clothing at her beauty salon nearly every day. Most women in Ivory Coast wear a **headdress** to match their dress.

My auntie fixes my hair in **cornrows**. This hairstyle began in Africa. She also styles my mother's hair.

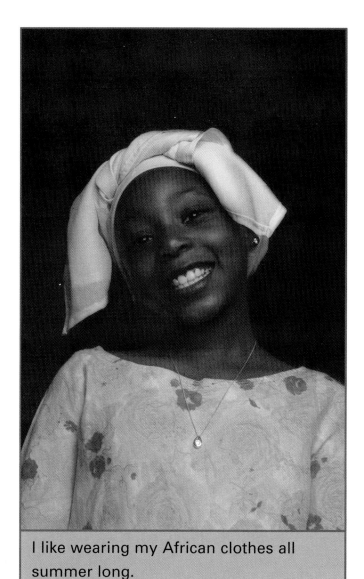

I like wearing my African clothes all summer long.

My grandmother in Africa **designs** and sews all my traditional clothes. I love getting packages from her in New York. These boxes always hold a special dress for me.

School Days

My mom and dad each have their own apartment. When I stay at my dad's apartment, I just have to walk a block to school. When I am at my mom's place, I take a bus or taxi.

In Ivory Coast, my school was not far from my grandparents' house. My grandparents are rich. Their driver takes people where they want to go. The driver or my grandpa would drive me to school.

I usually take a bus to school, like the one behind me here.

I love to read all kinds of books.

It was hard when I first came to school here. I did not speak any English, but I learned the language very quickly. Now I am at the top of my class.

The school here is different from my school in Ivory Coast. In Ivory Coast, I had one teacher who taught all our subjects. In New York, I have different teachers for different subjects.

In Ivory Coast, I used to raise one finger to talk to my teacher. In the United States, everyone raises their whole hand.

My favorite subject is math.

My tae kwon do teacher has me kick a paddle instead of kicking him. I have to aim carefully!

After school, I go to my **tae kwon do** class. I learn to defend myself in tae kwon do. I use different kicks and punches. I started taking tae kwon do lessons six months ago. I really love the classes.

I like doing my homework on my bed.

After my tae kwon do class, I come home and start my homework. Today, I am working on a science project. Science is one of my favorite subjects.

Faith and Family

Like many people in Ivory Coast, I am a **Muslim**. Muslims believe in Allah, or God.

In Ivory Coast, I prayed with my whole family. My grandpa used to lead us in prayer. The boys always stood in front, and the girls stood behind them. I stood next to my grandma.

In New York, I pray to Allah by myself or with my mom.

I made this Mother's Day card for my mom. I wrote it in English and in French.

Sometimes I would rather be in Africa with my grandparents in their big house. I liked my life in Ivory Coast better. There, people had time for me. Someone was always home for me. Here, my mom has to work very long hours. She cannot be with me as much as she would like to.

Many people in the United States think that Africa is full of wild animals. They think that everyone lives in huts in villages.

In Ivory Coast, the only place I saw wild animals was in a zoo. The only village I know is where my great-grandmother lives. She lives in a house with electricity, a television, and a cell phone. I try to teach my friends here about how people really live in Ivory Coast and Africa.

Just like in Ivory Coast, the only wild animals in New York City are in the zoo!

Glossary

cornrows — a style in which the hair is tightly braided in straight rows or in different patterns

designs — thinks up an original plan

grasslands — large areas of land covered with grasses and other short plants

headdress — a covering for the head

homeland — the country where someone comes from originally

ingredients — items that something is made from

Muslim — a believer in the religion of Islam

official — describes something approved by a government or other group

plantains — starchy fruits that are like bananas

Senegal — a country on the northwest coast of Africa

spicy — flavored with hot spices or herbs

tae kwon doe — a kind of martial art or self defense that started in Korea

traditional — based on custom or an older fashion

For More Information

Books

Cote D'Ivoire. Cultures of the World (series). Patricia Sheeha (Benchmark Books)

Ivory Coast in Pictures. Visual Geography Series. Janice Hamilton (Lerner Publications)

Stories from West Africa. Robert Hull (Raintree Publishers)

West Africa. Food & Festivals (series). Ali Brownlie Bojang (Raintree Publishers)

Web Sites

Cote d'Ivoire National Anthem

david.national-anthems.net/ci.htm

Click on this site to hear the national anthem of Ivory Coast

Publisher's note to educators and parents: Our editors have carefully reviewed this Web site to ensure that it is suitable for children. Many Web sites change frequently, however, and we cannot guarantee that a site's future contents will continue to meet our high standards of quality and educational value. Be advised that children should be closely supervised whenever they access the Internet.

Index

About the Author

Valerie Weber lives in Milwaukee, Wisconsin, with her husband and two daughters. She has been writing for children and adults for more than twenty-five years. She is grateful to both her family and friends for their support over that time. She would also like to thank the families who allowed her a glimpse of their lives for this series.